FOUR FAMISHED FOXES AND Fosdyke

BY PAMELA DUNCAN EDWARDS

ILLUSTRATED BY HENRY COLE

■ HarperCollins*Publishers*

In memory of my father, Harry Duncan,
who encouraged me to write.
And for Edith Edwards—Milly—the perfect mother-in-law.
With love —P.D.E.

For MOM, A.M., and A.P.R.
—H.C.

FOUR FAMISHED FOXES AND FOSDYKE
Text copyright © 1995 by Pamela Duncan Edwards
Illustrations copyright © 1995 by Henry Cole

Library of Congress Cataloging-in-Publication Data
Edwards, Pamela Duncan.
    Four famished foxes and Fosdyke / by Pamela Duncan Edwards ;
illustrated by Henry Cole.
        p.   cm.
    Summary: An alliterative tale about four foxes who go hunting in
the barnyard while their gourmet brother fixes a vegetarian feast.
    ISBN 0-06-024925-0. — ISBN 0-06-024926-9 (lib. bdg.)
    1. Foxes—Fiction.   I. Cole, Henry, ill.   II. Title.
PZ7.E26365Fo   1995   94-18700
[E]—dc20   CIP
                                                              AC

Typography by Elynn Cohen
3   4   5   6   7   8   9   10
❖

How many objects beginning with the
letter "F" can you find drawn in this book?
We counted at least 60. Can you do better?

Once down a foxhole lived a family of fox kits.
There was Frank, there was Floyd,
there were Freddy and Flo.

Fosdyke made five.

6

"Farewell," cried their fox mom. "I'm off
for five days in Florida. I feel you can now
find food for yourselves."

7

"What fun!" cried Frank. "We'll filch fowl from the farmyard."

"We're fierce! We're fearless!" agreed Floyd, Fred, and Flo.

"Frankly," said Fosdyke,
"I'm rather fond of French food."
"Flibbertigibbet!" yelled Flo.
"What a fool!" added Frank.
"What a failure to foxhood,"
the ferocious four cried.
"Fiddlesticks," said Fosdyke,
as he flambéed some fungi. "A
fox is a fox, whatever the food."

9

February 4
4:15 A.M.

The moon shone like a floodlight, as with furtive footsteps they crossed the field toward the farmyard.

COOP
SWEET
COOP

But oh, what a fracas faced the
flabbergasted felons. The fowl were
forewarned and began to fight back.
Four frantic foxes fled to their foxhole
to escape from the fray.

12

13

"I'm fainting," gasped Frank.
"I'm famished," whispered Flo.
"How did those featherbrained
fowl know we were near?"
"Don't tell Fosdyke,"
fussed Fred, "or he'll
know we have failed."

14

Fosdyke was frosting a flan
of fresh fruit.

"Fun hunting?" he asked.

"Fantastic!" they fibbed.

February 4
4:45 A.M.

The moon's light forged a path through the ferns to the farmyard.

Cried Frank, "Follow me. From the fight we'll not flinch. We are four fearsome foxes. Those fowl are just finks."

But Fergus the Foxhound soon finished their flimflam, as four fox tails lost fangfuls of fur. "Flee!" barked Fred to his frightened family. They flew from the farmyard as fast as they could.

"I'm fainting," gasped Frank.
"I'm famished," whispered Flo.
"How did those featherbrained
fowl know we were near?"
"Don't tell Fosdyke,"
fussed Fred, "or he'll
know we have failed."

Fosdyke was flavoring fritters
with a dressing of fiddleheads.
"Fun hunting?" he asked.
"Fantastic!" they fibbed.
The four little foxes were
flustered and fretful.
Said Fosdyke, "I'll make
some French fries for you."
"Fathead," screamed Flo.
"We're foxes, flesh eaters;
we don't eat French fries."
"I do," flipped Fosdyke.
"And also French toast."

21

February 4
5:15 A.M.

Fingers of moonlight fell on the foxes as they flitted once more toward the farmyard.

23

Suddenly up flashed the figure of the furious farmer. "Fiends," he fumed, with a fierce frown.

Frank flinched. Fred floundered. Flo fell flat
on her face. In a frantic frenzy the four of them fled.

26

Fosdyke was frying a pan of fresh figs. "Fun hunting?" he asked, flinging in fennel to taste.

"We're famished," they howled.
"We're fed up," they cried.
"We're finished with farmyards.
We've got to find food!"

"Fabulous," said Fosdyke.
"For I've made quite a feast."

27

"First-class food," said Frank.
"All my favorites," fawned Floyd.
"What fascinating flavors," cried Freddy and Flo.

28

"But," fretted Frank, "we're still failures and fakes. How did those flapdoodles figure out we were near?"

Said Fosdyke, "I feel I must tell you. It's foolish to forage when there's a FULL MOON."

29

In a flash the foxes faced up to their folly. "Why, funny old Fosdyke," the four of them cried, "how foxy of you to fathom that out." "Furthermore," said Fosdyke, "tomorrow's going to be foggy. I fancy you'll find that's a fine time to set forth. But in case fate's against you, I'll be fixing a fondue, and I'll make it a feast big enough to feed five."

February 5
5:15 A.M.

"For a fox is a fox, whatever the food."

F